W9-CHI-163

This book belongs to

Olivia..................

Copyright © 2019

make believe ideas ltd

The Wilderness, Berkhamsted, Hertfordshire, HP4 2AZ, UK.
501 Nelson Place, P.O. Box 141000, Nashville, TN 37214-1000, USA.

All rights reserved. No part of this publication may be reproduced,
stored in a retrieval system, or transmitted in any form or by any means,
electronic, mechanical, photocopying, recording, or otherwise, without
the prior written permission of the copyright owner.

www.makebelieveideas.com

Written by Rosie Greening.
Illustrated by Lara Ede.

Just
NARWHAL

Lara Ede • Rosie Greening

make
believe
ideas

Narwhal was a whale who thought she had **no skills** at all.

She couldn't **cook** . . .

Recipe

or knit...

or sing...

or even
catch a ball!

Meanwhile, all her **mermaid** friends were skillful as can be.
If they tried out something **new**, they did it **perfectly**.

"**Wow!**" thought Narwhal every day.
"There's nothing they can't do.
But I'm **just Narwhal**,
and I wish that I had **talent** too."

One morning, Star and Coral
cried to **Narwhal** in distress:

"Our **art contest** has started,
but everything's a **mess!**"

STAR

MARINA

"We need a **judge**," said Coral,
"and our time is nearly up.
Can **you** judge our paintings
and decide who wins this **cup?**"

SANDY

ISLA

CORAL

Narwhal thought,
"I'll get it wrong,"
and quickly shook her head.
She told them, "I'm just Narwhal –
I'll find someone else instead."

She asked **Cackle the Clownfish**
to decide which art should win.

ISLA

"The prize goes to the

FUNNIEST!"

said Cackle with a grin.

Narwhal thought,
"That's not enough to win the special prize.
But I'm **just Narwhal**, so I'll check
with someone **big** and **wise**."

She found a **big blue whale** and asked,
"Which painting is the **best?**"

"The
BIGGEST!"
shouted Jumbo.
"Forget about the rest!"

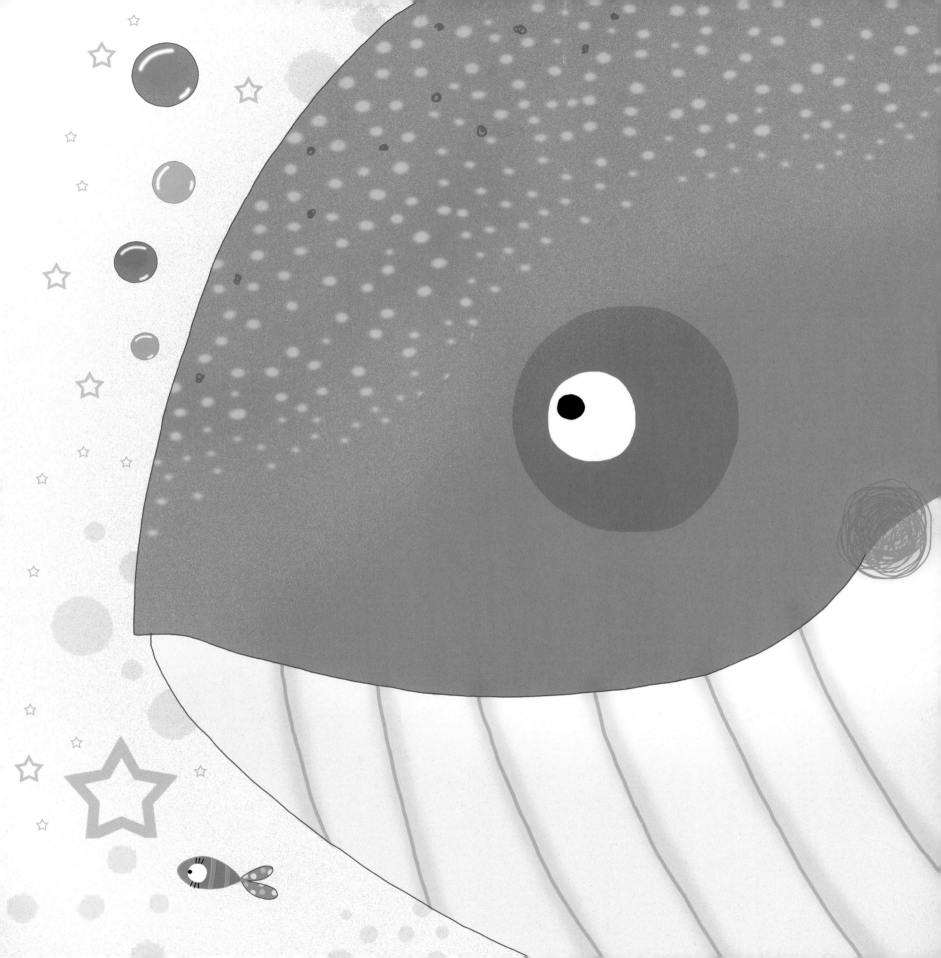

"I'm not sure size is **everything**," said Narwhal quietly.
"But since I am **just Narwhal**,
I'll make sure **Shelly** agrees."

Shelly scuttled around the art, but judged them **selfishly**.
The shellfish said, "The **winner** is the one that features . . .

ME!"

MARINA

Narwhal looked around and thought,
"These choices **don't** seem fair.

ISLA

CORAL

MARINA

They **can't** judge on **one thing** alone: there's **much** more to compare."

Narwhal swam to join her friends.
"I've let you down!" she cried.

"You need a **fair** and **honest** judge,
who sees how **hard** you tried."

The mermaids said, "If that's the case,
then **YOU** should judge our art!
To us, you're not '**just Narwhal**,'
and we'd **love** you to take part."

Narwhal gave a
nervous smile and said,
"Okay, I'll try!"

STAR

MARINA

ISLA

And she wrote a list of **qualities**
to judge the paintings by.

Narwhal swam around the art,
and **studied** each with care.
She looked at **every** brush stroke
to make sure that she was **fair**.

- Colors
- Theme
- Brushstroke
- Technique
- Effort
- Beauty

SANDY

At last she said, "Each piece of art
is **special** in its way.
But **ONE** checked every box for me . . .

Star wins first prize today!"

1ST

STAR

Star held up the shining cup
for **everyone** to see.
Then Coral rushed to Narwhal,
and she **hugged** her gratefully.

She said, "You are the **finest** judge
we could have ever found.
You're **fair** and **open-minded** . . .

the most **JUST** narwhal around!"

From that day on, **Narwhal** would judge
each contest she could find.

FINISH

And though she couldn't dance or sing, at last, she didn't **mind**.

She thought,

"My **skills** are hidden –
they're not **obvious** to see.
But just like all the **paintings**,

there is so much
more to me!"